Alice held out her hand. There were three letters for her father, and a small, box-shaped parcel addressed to – herself!

'Hey!' she cried. 'Look! It's for me! And it's not even my birthday!'

Alice's excitement soon fades when she sees the contents of the mysterious box. Why on earth would Great Aunt Alice want her to have a funny old bottle and some ancient, very unappetizing, bits of food? But Greedy Alice can't resist just a tiny taste . . .

BY MYSELF books are specially selected to be suitable for beginner readers. Other BY MYSELF books available from Young Corgi Books include:

E.S.P. by Dick King-Smith
THE LITTLE DRAGON STEPS OUT by Ann Jungman
URSULA EXPLORING by Sheila Lavelle
PURR by Jennifer Zabel
DRAGON AIR by Ann Ruffell
MIKE'S MAGIC SEEDS by Alexander McCall Smith

GREEDY ALICE

HELEN CRESSWELL

GREEDY ALICE

Illustrated by Kate Simpson

YOUNG CORGI BOOKS

GREEDY ALICE

A YOUNG CORGI BOOK 0 552 525243

Originally published in Great Britain in 1986 by
Marilyn Malin Books in association with André Deutsch Ltd.
Based on original design by Belitha Press.

PRINTING HISTORY

Marilyn Malin Books / André Deutsch edition published 1986
Young Corgi edition published 1989

This book is set in 14/18 pt Garamond
by Colset Private Limited, Singapore.

Young Corgi Books are published by Transworld Publishers Ltd., 61–63 Uxbridge Road, Ealing, London W5 5SA, in Australia by Transworld Publishers (Australia) Pty. Ltd., 15–23 Helles Avenue, Moorebank, NSW 2170, and in New Zealand by Transworld Publishers (N.Z.) Ltd., Cnr. Moselle and Waipareira Avenues, Henderson, Auckland.

Made and printed in Great Britain by
The Guernsey Press Co. Ltd, Guernsey
Channel Islands

GREEDY ALICE

Chapter 1

The main two things you need to know about Alice are that she was greedy and a show-off. (She was also bossy, untidy and good-tempered, but none of that really matters to the story.)

This is how greedy she was. At Christmas

she would find bags of chocolate coins and tins of sweets in her stocking. I expect you think I am going to say that she had gobbled them all up by the time for Christmas dinner. Not at all. Not our Alice. She would get her little sister Kate to open *her* chocolates, and eat those, so that she still had all her own left. After that she would still manage at least two helpings of turkey and stuffing and sausage and roast potatoes and sprouts and peas and good thick gravy. She was not very fond of Christmas pudding, so she would then have some more of Kate's chocolate instead.

If someone opened a bag of crisps at school, Alice's hand would go diving in twice as often as anyone else's. People

often went behind corners to open bags of crisps when Alice was around. If someone was passing round a bottle of pop, Alice would always take a mighty swig. She would glurp and glurp till she was red in the face.

'Why don't you swallow the bottle while you're at it?' her friends would ask.

As for showing off, she did that the whole time. In the choir she sang twice as loudly as anyone else (and flat as a pancake, too). At Sports Day, when she saw that she was not going to win the race (probably because she was stuffed full with crisps and pop), she pretended to fall. She lay on the ground and moaned and groaned.

'My leg! I've broken my leg!'

Everyone ran up to help her. Nobody took any notice at all of the poor boy who won the race.

But one day Alice's greediness and showing-off got her into very big trouble.

It was a perfectly ordinary day to begin with. Alice came down to breakfast. She filled a large bowl with cereal and started to shovel it down, between slurps of tea.

'For the millionth time, Alice,' said her mother, 'it is not ladylike to gobble and slurp. You must learn to nibble and sip if you want to be a lady.'

'I don't!' replied Alice. 'Nibble and sip, my foot! Is my bacon and egg ready yet? I'm ravenous!'

Just then she looked out of the window and saw her best friend, Sue.

'Back in a tick!' she said, pushing away her empty bowl.

She went out and on to the grass that ran in front of the high block of flats.

'Hi, Sue!' she called, and promptly stood on her head. This was the latest of her show-offs, and she did it all the time. She had even tried to do it in the bath.

Sue came over.

'You look better that way up,' she said.

Alice came back the right way up. For a moment the trees and the tower blocks of flats rocked and spun.

'I'm going ice-skating later on,' Sue told her. 'Coming?'

'I'll ask Mum.' Alice hoped the answer would be yes. The ice-rink was a very good place to show off. She wondered if she could stand on her head on the ice? She thought probably not.

'It might freeze my brains,' she thought.

'Here – want to take these?' It was the postman. 'Save my poor old legs.'

Alice held out her hand. There were three letters for her father, and a small, box-shaped parcel addressed to – herself!

'Hey!' she cried. 'Look! It's for me! And it's not even my birthday!'

She ran off to look for scissors.

'Call on me later!' she shouted to Sue.

Sue lived on the very top floor of the block, and often wished she had wings.

Alice rushed back into the kitchen.

'Look at this, look at this!' She held up the parcel. 'For me! A surprise! Where are the scissors?'

Chapter 2

Next minute the string was cut and the paper was torn away. Inside was a box, a very old one. The colours on the lid had nearly worn away. There was a letter, too. Alice read it quickly.

'It says that Great Aunt Alice has died,'

she told the others. 'And she's left this box to me. Is that the Alice I was named after?'

'There have always been Alices in our family,' said her mother.

Alice picked up the box and shook it.

'There's something inside! Gold coins! Diamonds!'

'*Not* very likely,' said her father.

'Oh!' Alice had the box open, and let out a gasp of disappointment.

She saw an old-fashioned bottle of green glass with a cork stopper, and two other, smaller boxes. She picked up the bottle and peered at the faint letters on the label.

'DRINK ME,' she read. 'Ugh! Whatever is it, do you think?'

'It seems a funny thing to *leave* to

somebody, in a will,' said her mother.

'I bet it's poison,' said Kate. 'Go on, drink it!'

Alice aimed a slap at her, but missed. She picked up one of the smaller boxes and read the label on that.

'EAT ME.' She opened the box. Inside was a kind of biscuit, or dried-up cake.

'It's second-hand!' she said in disgust. 'A second-hand biscuit!'

Somebody had certainly been nibbling at it. She opened the second box. That was even more disappointing. Inside that was a single mushroom, or even a toadstool, for all she knew. Luckily a plate of bacon and egg was then put in front of her.

'We're going straight off to do the

shopping after breakfast,' her mother told her. 'So you'll stop here and keep an eye on Kate.'

'Oh *Mum!* I wanted to go ice-skating with Sue!'

'We shan't take long,' Mum said.

As soon as breakfast was cleared away, off they went.

'And no fancy tricks while we've gone!' warned Dad.

Little did he know that Alice was going to do the fanciest trick of her whole life. And she was going to do it without even meaning to.

'I want to skip!' said Kate.

So they went outside and Alice sat on the warm grass with a book and her box. Then Sue came over.

'If you wait for me, I can go skating later,' Alice told her. 'Here, look at this! It's been left to me in a will!'

Sue peered into the old box and pulled a face.

'Ugh! What is it? Just an old bottle and a bit of old cake. And who wants a mushroom?'

This annoyed Alice.

'It may look like that,' she said. 'But it's very important, and very valuable.'

She took the box back, and noticed for the first time a piece of folded paper at the bottom. She pulled it out. It was crisp and yellow and very old. Alice suddenly gave a little shiver under the hot sun.

'What does it say?' Sue asked.

Alice frowned.

'It says: THIS IS STRONG MAGIC. REMEMBER WHAT HAPPENED TO ME. GO TIPTOE. BEWARE!'

'What does *that* mean?' asked Sue.

'What *did* happen?'

'I don't know,' said Alice.

'Anyway, I think what it means is *don't* eat it, and *don't* drink it,' Sue said. 'It's a warning.'

'Pooh!' said Alice. 'I think I will, and see what happens.'

She couldn't resist showing *she* wasn't scared.

Which should she try first? The mixture in the bottle did look rather like poison. On the other hand, the cake looked very second-hand. But she didn't like mushrooms even cooked, let alone uncooked.

'Eeny meeny miney mo,' she remarked. 'I think I'll have a bite of that cake.'

She picked it up. Being Alice, she took not a nibble, but one of her usual great big bites.

'There's no such thing as magic, anyway!' she said.

Chapter 3

Famous last words!

'There's no such thing as magic!'

What, then, was happening? Almost at once she had the strangest feeling. It was as if she were going up fast in a lift, except that she herself was the lift. She was stretching, soaring, zooming.

'Oooooeeeh!' she screamed. 'Ooooeeeh!'

The walls and windows of the tower block rushed past her. She thought she must be going to the moon.

'Stop!' screamed Alice. 'Stop!' . . . though she did not really know who she was saying it to.

But now the lift did not seem to be going quite so fast. It was definitely slowing down.

'Hey – get away, giant!'

Alice saw a boy from school, Tommy Bates, jumping up and down on a balcony.

'It's *me!*' screamed Alice. 'It's Alice!'

'Yah! Can't be.'

'Oh, can't it?' she said, and reached

over and picked him up.

He squirmed and wriggled in that enormous fist.

'*Is* it me?' she demanded. 'Or shall I drop you? Splat!'

'Oooh, oooh, it *is* you, Alice!'

She held him between her enormous first finger and thumb.

'Say sorry, then.'

'S-s-sorry!' he squeaked. 'Sorry sorry sorry sorry – oh!'

She plonked him back on to the balcony. (The trouble is, though, that it was the wrong one. Alice was still growing, and this balcony was five floors higher up.)

Tommy ran straight into what he thought was his own flat, and then ran back out, quick as a flash.

'You clear out! What're you doing in here?'

A red-faced man ran out after Tommy, shaking his fist.

'*She* put me here!' yelled Tommy Bates.

The man saw Alice. His jaw dropped.

'Goodbye!' she called. 'Still going up!'

She stuck out her enormous red tongue.

She *was* still going up, though more and more slowly. At last she did stop. She turned her head to find that it was now level with the very top of the block of flats. Then, for the first time, she looked down. She could see the tiny figures of Kate and Sue, and hear their faint cries.

'Oooh!' quavered Alice. 'I feel dizzy!'

The cars and buses looked like toys. Even her own feet seemed a mile away. They did not seem to belong to her at all. She could see people swarming on to the grass like ants. A crowd was gathering.

'It must be a nightmare!' thought Alice.

'I'll wake up soon.'

She was a show-off. She liked people to look at her. But this was going too far.

Above the faint shouts down below she heard other, louder voices. She turned her head and saw faces poking from the windows and balconies of the flats.

'Alice!' She heard a voice she knew. 'It's Alice Brown, from downstairs!'

There, only a few feet away from her eyes, were Sue's mother and father.

'Whatever do you think you're doing?' said Mrs Drake sharply. 'Little show-off!'

'Not so little,' said Mr Drake.

'Get down at once!' went on his wife. 'Go away! Shoo!'

'I can't, I can't,' wailed Alice. 'Oooh,

I'm dizzy. I want to sit down.'

'Don't you dare!' said Mrs Drake. 'You'd squash everybody. Our Sue's down there. She'd be squashed like an ant. Don't even move your great big feet, do you hear?'

Alice began to cry. She looked down and saw that people were putting up umbrellas.

'I'm a shower!' she thought. 'I'm a rain storm!' and she cried even more.

Then through her tears she saw flashing blue lights. She heard the faint wail of a siren.

'Oh, thank goodness,' she cried. 'It's the fire brigade! They've come to fetch me down!'

She had read about the fire brigade rescuing kittens from high trees. She wasn't exactly a kitten, she knew, but there must be something they could do . . .

Chapter 4

As it happened, there was. The Fire Chief himself came to her rescue. Way down below, Sue and Kate showed him the box Alice had been given.

'Ah *ha!*' remarked the Fire Chief.

He was a big, red-faced man with

whiskers, but he had once been a child himself. And when he *was* a child, his favourite book had been *Alice's Adventures in Wonderland*. So he knew at once what was going on.

'Leave this to me, men!' he ordered.

He took the box.

'I'm going up!' he said.

'Please, Sir, the lift's broken,' Sue told him. 'It nearly always is!'

So the Fire Chief went up on the turntable. It didn't quite reach the top of the building, so he got out and climbed the last few flights of stairs. There he went into Mr and Mrs Drake's flat and poked his head out of the window.

'I've come to get you down,' he told

Alice. 'Just look at your eyes – as big as dustbin lids!'

'That's a very rude thing to say!' sobbed Alice.

'Do stop crying,' he told her, 'or the boys will have to get the pumps out.'

Alice sniffed and gulped. She did feel rather large to be a cry baby.

'Now, take this,' said the Fire Chief, 'and drink some.'

He held out his hand. Alice looked. It was the old green glass bottle. Alice's huge hand came up to meet his. The Fire Chief placed the bottle very carefully in a palm the size of a tablecloth. She lifted it to her mouth.

'Steady!' shouted the Fire Chief.

'Careful! Don't gulp it – *sip!*'

Too late! Alice's head went back and every drop went down her long, long throat. The whole bottle very nearly went with it.

'Wheeee!'

Down Alice shot, like a shooting star. Walls and windows rushed past. A deafening roar filled her ears.

She came to a stop with a jolt.

'Oh!' she gasped. Then, 'Where am I?'

She seemed to be among thin green spears as high as her waist. It was the grass. She looked about, and saw giant boulders and mountains. They were moving. They were *shoes!*

'Don't tread on me, don't tread on me!' she begged. Her voice was a tiny squeak.

Above her voices were bellowing.

'Where is she? Where's she gone? Don't move! She must be here somewhere!'

'W-what if she's v-vanished altogether!' Alice heard Kate wail.

'I'm here, I'm here!' she screamed. She might as well have been a mouse squeaking.

One of the boulders, red and white, was Kate's foot, she felt. A shoelace was trailing, so Alice caught hold of it. Up she swarmed like a monkey. She climbed and climbed till she was sitting on top of the shoe. At least she felt safer there.

'I'll stop here,' thought Alice. 'If I stop here long enough, she'll bend down to tie up her laces. Then she'll see me. And if she *doesn't* see me, I'll pull her laces untied again! I'll do it a *million* times, till she does see me!'

And so Alice hung grimly on to the shoelace, and waited.

Chapter 5

'Stand still! Stand still!' Alice heard the Fire Chief shout. 'Alice, where are you?'

'Here!' she squeaked. 'Here!'

No one could hear her.

'*I* know what I'll do,' thought Alice. 'I'll show them I'm here! I'll tie Kate's shoelaces together. Then, when she moves, she'll fall flat on her face!'

So that is what she did. It was not easy. Kate's shoelaces seemed as thick as rope to Alice's tiny fingers.

'It'd be just my luck,' thought Alice, 'if

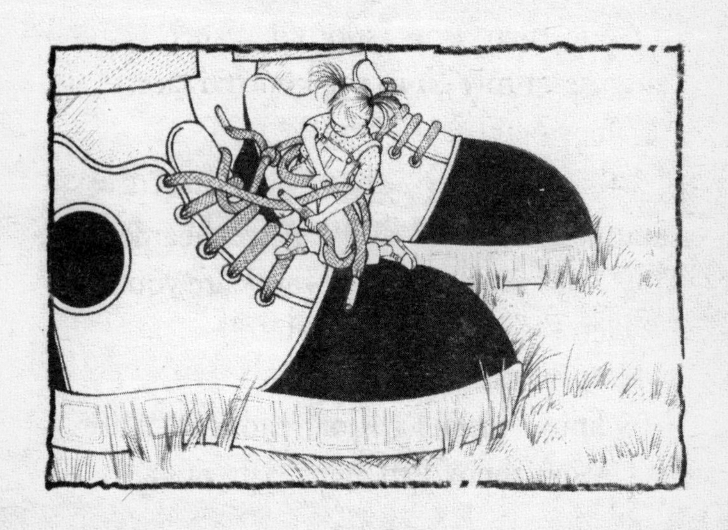

when she falls, she falls on me and squashes me flat! But I'll have to risk it.'

No sooner had she tied the lace of the right shoe to that of the left than Kate moved – and tripped and fell.

'Oooh!' she screamed. 'Who's – ? What's – ?'

And then she spotted Alice, still hanging grimly on to the knotted laces.

'She's here! She's here!'

'Ah *ha!*' said the Fire Chief. '*Here* we are! You stand still, Kate. Don't move your feet, or she might slip off and hurt herself. Everyone else stand back.'

He got down on his hands and knees. Now *his* eyes looked as big as dustbin lids, to poor shrunken Alice.

'I told you not to gulp!' he said severely. 'One more drop, and you'd have vanished altogether.'

'Oh help me, help me!' begged Alice.

'I'm going to try,' he told her. 'It's lucky we've got the mushroom.'

'But I don't *like* mushrooms!' wailed Alice. 'I don't even like them *cooked*, and that one's raw!'

'Do you mean to tell me that you have never read *Alice in Wonderland*?'

The Fire Chief was shocked. He thought everyone in the world had read it at least once, if not fifty times, like himself.

'There's only that mushroom can save you now, my girl,' he told her. 'Do you want to stop the size of a caterpillar all your life?'

'Oh no! Oh no!' sobbed Alice. 'I'll eat the mushroom. I'll eat anything!'

'You'll *nibble*, young lady,' the Fire Chief told her. 'Not that you've got much choice at the moment, the size you are.'

He held out the mushroom. To Alice it looked the size of Buckingham Palace.

'Now listen very carefully,' he said.

He told her what she must do.

'You must nibble the left-hand side first,' he said. 'That will shoot you up. If you go too far, you must straightaway nibble the right-hand side. You do know your left hand from your right?'

'Oh yes,' said Alice meekly.

'Right!' said the Fire Chief. 'Off you go, then. And remember – don't gobble – *nibble!*'

Alice took a deep breath and sank her tiny teeth into the left side of the mushroom.

It was a big bite. It was lucky she was so tiny, or she could easily have ended up sky high again. As it was, she found herself as high as a tree.

The crowd gasped. Alice looked down at their upturned faces. All her life she had longed to show off to a crowd as big as this. Now, she wished she could sink through a hole in the ground.

'Alice! Alice, whatever are you up to?'

She heard a familiar voice and saw, just by her right foot, her own mother and father. She bent down and picked them up, one in each hand.

They struggled and yelled.

'Put us down, put us down!'

'Oh Mum, oh Dad, what shall I do?' she cried, clutching them in her great fists.

'Tell her to pick up the mushroom and nibble!' yelled the Fire Chief. 'Doesn't she

know the *meaning* of the word nibble?'

'No,' said Alice's mother. 'She doesn't. She never has.'

'Then she'd better learn,' roared the Fire Chief. 'She'd better learn quickly, or goodness knows what size she'll end up!'

And so Alice Brown learned how to nibble. First a little at one side of the mushroom, then at the other. First she shrank, then she grew again. Until, at last . . .

'Ah!' gasped the crowd. 'That's it! She's done it!'

Alice looked wonderingly about her. The world had gone usual again. Everything was exactly the size it should be. And that was lucky, because she had just swallowed the very last of the mushroom.

'Now we can all go home,' said the Fire Chief.

And so they did. Alice kept the boxes for the rest of her life. She framed the old paper that said:

THIS IS STRONG MAGIC. REMEMBER WHAT HAPPENED TO ME. GO TIPTOE. BEWARE!

She hung it in her room, and every now and then would look at it, and say,

'And remember what happened to *me!*'

The very thought made her shudder. From that day on she never showed off again. She did not gobble, she nibbled. She did not gulp, she sipped. She read and re-read *Alice's Adventures in Wonderland* until she knew it almost by heart.

But secretly, in her heart of hearts, she thought her adventures were *much* more exciting.

THE END

E.S.P.

BY DICK KING-SMITH
ILLUSTRATED BY PETER WINGHAM

Old Smelly, the tramp, can hardly believe his luck when he meets young Eric Stanley Pigeon in the park. For the pigeon appears to have a very unusual talent – he can peck out the name of the winning horse from a list of runners in the newspapers. How does he do it? Could he possibly have . . . Extra Sensory Perception? E.S.P.?

0 552 525235

THE LITTLE DRAGON STEPS OUT

BY ANN JUNGMAN
ILLUSTRATED BY MAGGIE KNEEN

Janet gets a terrible shock when the Little Dragon she has been reading about steps out of her library book, and tells her he has a big problem.

If he goes back into the book, the Little Dragon will be killed by Sir George, a brave but old-fashioned Knight who thinks he must slay a dragon if he is to marry the beautiful Princess. Somehow Janet must help all the characters to work out a new story if the Little Dragon is to be saved . . .

0 552 525219